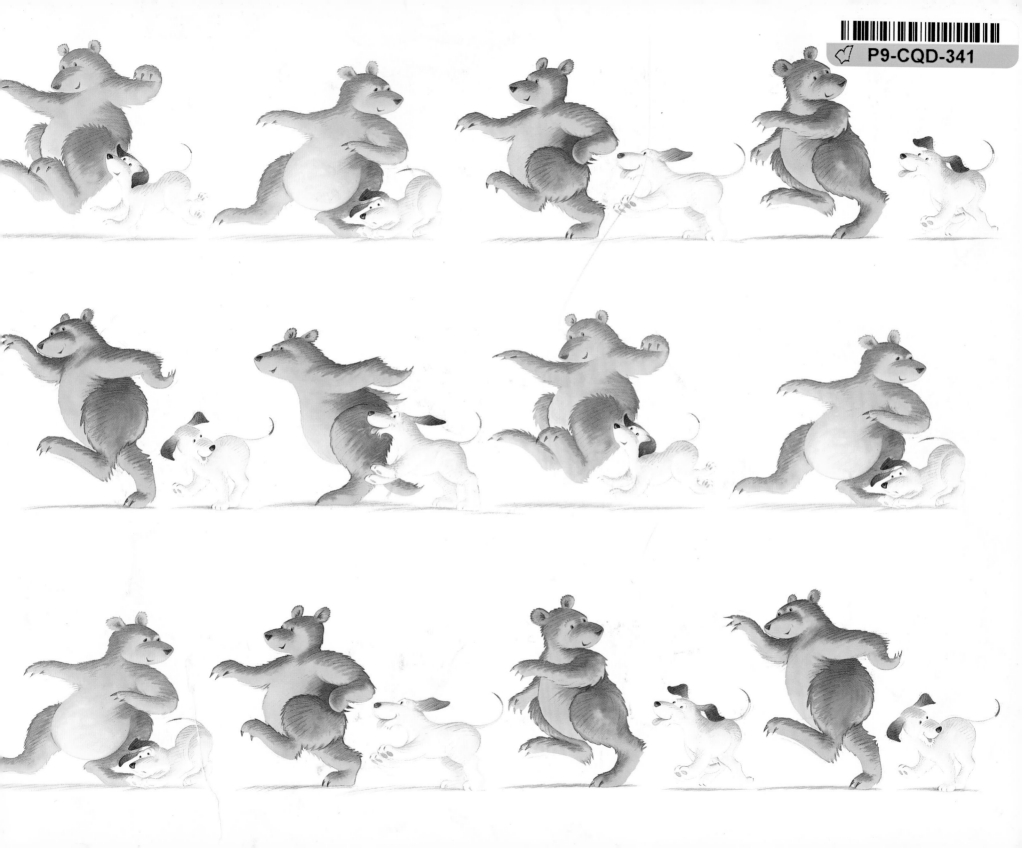

For bouncy bears everywhere!

CIP Data is available.

Published in the United States 1997 by Dutton Children's Books,
a division of Penguin Books USA Inc.
375 Hudson Street, New York, New York 10014

Originally published in Great Britain 1997 by
Ragged Bears, Limited, Hampshire, England

Typography by Ellen M. Lucaire
Printed in Singapore
First Edition
1 2 3 4 5 6 7 8 9 10
ISBN 0-525-45802-6

One Bear,
One Dog

PAUL STICKLAND

Dutton Children's Books • New York

One bear,

one dog,

one mouse,

one

frog,

one

kitten,

one

goose,

one

monkey,

one

moose,

one

beetle,

one

bee,

one

iger and...

ME!